The Curvatures of HURT

A Companion Edition to
the Audiobook featuring Jenny Bacon

Praise for Ted Morrissey's Fiction

Crowsong for the Stricken

"There's always a sense something is coming for his characters, although Morrissey never defines it clearly. Indeed, they never seem to be able to truly define their own unease—even as the author makes readers feel it, too."   — *Kirkus Reviews* (starred review)

"Absolutely enchanted by the story and its unique premise."   — *Flyleaf Journal*

An Untimely Frost

"Moments of true brilliance . . . reads like it was written by a postmodernist emulating Henry James, which proves to be an intriguing combination . . . The writing is in turns funny and harrowing."
                    — William Wright, *Chicago Book Review*

"The writing is beautiful and elaborate . . . It feels like a Victorian novel."   — Cecile Sune, *Book Obsessed*

"The novel becomes an engrossing mystery . . . a wonderful read that draws the reader in."
                    — Anne Drolet, *North American Review*

Men of Winter

"An engrossing odyssey along the edge of the world in which strange figures emerge . . . then mysteriously ebb back into the wartime ether."
                    — M. R. Branwen, *Slush Pile Magazine*

The Curvatures of Hurt

A Crowsong Universe Story

Ted Morrissey

With an Afterword by Jenny Bacon

Twelve Winters Press

Published by Twelve Winters Press, a literary publisher.

P. O. Box 414 • Sherman, Illinois 62684-0414 • twelvewinters. com/contact

The Curvatures of Hurt was published by Twelve Winters Press in 2018 and is also available in digital and audio editions. *The Curvatures of Hurt* also appeared as part of *Crowsong for the Stricken* in 2017, in hardcover, paperback and digital editions. All are available from Twelve Winters Press.

Cover and interior pages by TWP Design.

The cover image is from the Williamsville (Illinois) High School yearbook for 1957.

ISBN
978-0-9987057-3-6
Printed in the United States of America

Acknowledgments

"The Curvatures of Hurt" first appeared at *Fiction on the Web*, edited by Charlie Fish. It was later published as part of *Crowsong for the Stricken*. My appreciation to Pamm Collebrusco for her able assistance in editing the book-length manuscript, and also to Jenny Bacon for her haunting vocal work on the audiobook of *Curvatures*, as well as for writing this edition's Afterword.

for Melissa

The Curvatures of Hurt

What is friendship?

A single soul dwelling in two bodies.

—ARISTOTLE

A

WINTER HAD LINGERED INTO SPRING, and patches of heavy, wet snow were melting in the cold sunshine as Frankie walked with urgency toward Shirley Donaldson's. Water ran in the gutters beneath disappearing canopies of ice. It was mid-afternoon on a Saturday, the sort of day Frankie and Rebecca would have spent entirely together not long ago, one of them having slept at the other's house. She had not heard from Rebecca since they left school the day before, with Rebecca hurrying because she wanted to get a jump on her homework, she said.

More and more, Rebecca was at Shirley Donaldson's house. Rebecca and Shirley had been friends before Frankie moved to the village, but Frankie's impression was that Rebecca barely cared for Shirley's company. Frankie didn't care for her company. Yet when Frankie knocked on the Phillipses' door and Pastor Phillips, who always called her Miss Francine, said that his daughter was at Shirley's, Frankie was consumed by emotions that drove her to visit the Donaldsons too.

Frankie stood on their porch and knocked on the storm-door. No one came. She went back to the walk which led to the porch and turned around to look up at Shirley's bedroom window: She recalled the one time she'd been in Shirley's room, with Rebecca, and looking out the window in utter boredom and seeing the walk (then, with everything in the steamy green of summer foliage). Peering back, now, the bedroom curtain was drawn, and the window—the whole two-story house—was a sickly shade of pale. Frankie listened carefully, patient through spikes of chill wind, and perhaps there were voices to be heard ... muffled and distant. She couldn't help seeking them, so she began treading through the yard's soft snow, around the side of the house, past the dormant forsythia bush, the voices becoming louder but only slightly so.

Frankie reached a point where the inarticulate voices were loudest. Frankie stood quietly, her mittened hands in her coat pockets, listening, and one of the voices was definitely Rebecca's. She couldn't say for certain that the other voice was Shirley's—something about it didn't seem right, its cadence, and its pitch perhaps, sounding almost like a boy's or a young man's even.

They were muffled through the basement window at Frankie's feet. Jealousy swelled in her. When she heard Rebecca's voice again, she squatted and knocked on the window. It wasn't covered, and incandescent light fell in a yellow patch upon the pane. The voices ceased. Frankie removed a mitten and rapped more sharply. A face appeared in the window, Rebecca's. It held so many emotions at once it seemed distorted, and Frankie barely recognized her best friend—*best friend*, that was how Frankie called her, but the phrase didn't seem adequate to their relationship, not to how it had been since the end of summer. Yet lately they had slipped back beyond that inadequate phrase to barely friends at all.

For a moment they stared back and forth through the small window, Rebecca looking up, in a supplicant's posture, her willful brown hair framing her narrow white face.

Let me in, said Frankie, motioning toward the front of the house with the bare hand holding its mitten.

Rebecca's face disappeared from the window, and

Frankie went to the front porch to wait for her. Standing there, hands in her coat, she tried to sort through her emotions, which were myriad, sometimes complementary, sometimes conflicting—many inexpressible. She wanted to cling to the happiness she felt at seeing Rebecca, but anger, hurt and jealousy kept elbowing their way into her heart.

She waited on the porch several interminable minutes but no one came to let her in. She returned to the side of the house: the basement was perfectly silent, and even the patch of electric light had disappeared from the pane.

B

REBECCA PHILLIPS WAITED ANXIOUSLY in the corner. She knew that Frankie wouldn't give up easily. Her stubbornness was one of the first qualities she admired in her friend, but now it complicated things. Frankie must be upset. There was no help for it though. Shirley had reached out and shared something extraordinary with her because they had been friends for as long as either could recall, and Rebecca wasn't the sort to gossip . . . *and* Rebecca was Pastor Phillips's daughter, which meant something, to be connected to God in such a special way.

Overhead, the floorboards of the porch creaked as Frankie impatiently shifted her weight, waiting for her to appear at the door and invite her inside. For a long while she had stared up at her best friend through the dirty basement window, torn about what to do, wishing that Frankie hadn't tracked her down.

Frankie went to be let in the front door, and Shirley pulled the cord to extinguish the basement lights. Then Shirley spoke in the voice that was queerly edged: Rafael says we must wait here until she leaves us alone.

In a few minutes, Frankie returned to the spot by the window, and Rebecca watched her friend's boots and the legs of her black corduroy slacks—Rebecca safe from sight in the basement's obscurity. Finally Frankie left.

There, said Shirley. Rafael says Frankie mustn't know. We can only trust you—for now at least. What? . . . All right, yes, John disagrees . . . Yes, *Shout from the mountain top*. But, John, you are a minority of one.

Shirley was only a few feet away from Rebecca in the basement's gray light, and Rebecca searched the gloom for John and Rafael and the others—the number always varying because the angels came and went of their own accord, save for Rafael, who was Shirley's guardian and had been at her side these many months. The moment Rafael let his guard down, Anthony threatened to come, and Anthony meant her harm—not all angels were good and kind. In fact, they were as varied in their personalities as people. Sometimes, in poor lighting, Rebecca thought she saw dim, ill-defined figures around Shirley but only for the briefest of moments.

Shirley went to the table and chairs that were in the corner of the basement. Come on, she said to Rebecca, we must finish our game.

Do you think it's all right to turn on the lights?

Shirley listened for a moment . . . No, not just yet. Rafael will say when. What? . . . Yes, Marcus prefers the dark—his eyes can't get used to electric light.

They went to the card table that was pushed into a corner of the basement allowing space for only two to sit. A half deck of playing cards was stacked in the center of the table, surrounded by the remainder of the deck laid in a pattern of Rafael's choosing, by directing Shirley's hand. Meanwhile he would speak the meaning of the cards and their patterns in Shirley's ear—sometimes she would share his words with Rebecca, sometimes not, only nod and take another card from the deck.

They sat at the table, on metal folding chairs, and Shirley took a card. Light came through the small window directly above the table. Shirley shared the card over her shoulder with Rafael and whoever else may be watching.

She listened to him, then allowed his words to guide her hand. She placed the nine of hearts at the end of the queen of clubs. Rafael explained its significance, and Shirley took another card, repeating the process with the three of spades, then the jack of spades. Finally she shared what Rafael had been telling her:

Henry lingers in his field, lonely, until he must look for comfort. He's creating all manner of mischief.

Rebecca wanted to ask what Rafael meant but knew to hold her tongue. Prodding only interrupted.

Miranda, Mary, Julie, Patricia, Sarah, Dorothy, Gloria . . . Frankie.

But that can't be.

Shirley tried to ignore the intrusion.

That can't be.

Shirley had taken a new card and was sharing it with Rafael.

What do you mean *making mischief*?

Irritated, Shirley looked at Rebecca. Maybe he'll tell us if we're patient. She looked toward the basement's gloom. Rafael, come back. She's sorry for butting in . . . aren't you sorry? Tell him, Rebecca.

Rebecca looked into the basement of shadows. Everything was so confusing. When Shirley confided in her that she spoke with angels, that they came to her at night especially but sought her at other times too, that one angel who called himself Rafael never left her—Rebecca wanted to believe. She had been surrounded by ideas of God and Jesus and the Virgin birth and the stories in the Bible her entire life, maybe surrounded by them more than anyone in the village since her father was the pastor, but for a long time she'd wondered . . . she didn't see signs of the Trinity anywhere, other than when adults said this or that was God's doing, something loving or something cruel, then

10

some adult, oftentimes her father, would ascribe it to God's love or God's mercy or God's wisdom. But the reasoning always struck Rebecca as convenient, even when she was a little girl. She wanted to ask her father and sometimes did, but his answers were hardly answers at all, and he clearly didn't approve of her curiosity. Then she met Frankie, who was so smart and sure of herself. Frankie didn't seem to believe, not with her whole heart, but she was willing to fit in, and soon the church and its functions were opportunities for her and Rebecca to be together. On Saturday nights, Frankie began sleeping over, sharing Rebecca's small bed, so that they could ready themselves for church and walk there together, just the two of them. Rebecca's father and mother would've left the house an hour before to prepare for the service.

Then one day Shirley asked Rebecca to come home with her after school, just her—and when they were alone in Shirley's room, she told Rebecca about the angels and introduced her to Rafael and Marcus, and swore her to secrecy.

Rafael and Marcus were older angels, especially Rafael, who was from another place altogether and spoke with an accent. Marcus was from a past time to be sure, but not nearly so past and so foreign as Rafael—yet it was Marcus who was pained by so many modern things: electric light, the ringing of the telephone, the thump of the needle on her records when Shirley played her phonograph, the backfiring of Mr. Finch's delivery truck. That evening Shirley described the whole catalog of angels who'd been visiting her, including Anthony, the angel who'd tried to pull her hair and seemed to want to strangle her. Rafael protected her and sent Anthony away and said he would need to be watchful because Anthony would try to return.

Rebecca sat on Shirley's bed for a long time listening.

At first she tried to ask questions but it was clear Shirley didn't want to answer questions—they hindered the flow of words she needed to speak. She'd obviously been keeping them dammed up for months, and now they were all pushing forth because Rebecca was there to listen. The angels told Shirley things about the village and about their neighbors, bits of gossip she'd never known but it was impossible to be sure if any of it was true. Shirley's story was fantastic, yet Rebecca wanted to believe. It would validate all the fantastic stories in the Bible, especially the ones about angels—Gabriel's visiting Mary, Michael's rescuing Daniel—and life would be better, simpler, if she believed with her whole heart as her father and mother did, as the entire village did.

Shirley must have sensed that her friend wasn't fully convinced. Rafael has told me something about *you*. Shirley's usually pale face was flushed, and her eyes were round and a little wild looking. The whole time she'd been speaking she held one of her bed pillows to her chest, gripping it fiercely.

About me? said Rebecca, from the foot of the bed, her legs folded beneath the spread of her wool skirt. What did he say?

Shirley hesitated. Perhaps I shouldn't tell you. She blinked and shifted the pillow in her hands. The pillowcase was crushed with the impression of her fingers.

Tell me.

She seemed to regain her momentum. Rafael says you've begun.

Begun, repeated Rebecca, knowing.

Yes, begun. Begun begun. You're a woman now.

It's not true . . .

Rebecca left Shirley's house that evening, sworn to secrecy, which almost wasn't necessary. She was so bewildered by Shirley's news that she would've had difficulty telling it to anyone, even to Frankie, who couldn't possibly accept the angels' existence. Rebecca was having trouble, too, even though she very much wanted to believe in them.

Γ

FRANKIE DIDN'T ATTEND SERVICES the morning after she'd been left standing on Shirley's porch. She didn't try to see Rebecca at all that day. Pastor Phillips didn't mention Frankie's absence. He must've noticed that Rebecca and Frankie's friendship had seemed to cool these last few weeks. Rebecca imagined that he was most concerned about how the state of their friendship affected Frankie's faith. If he noticed his daughter's anxiousness, he probably would've attributed it to her rift with Frankie. For that matter, when she thought of it, her father had seemed distracted too.

At school, Mrs. Wilson was teaching them about Homer's *Odyssey*, and that Monday they were reading and discussing the hero's journey to the underworld. *His communion with shades*, Mrs. Wilson called it. Every so often Rebecca would glance across the room toward Frankie, both hoping and fearing to catch her eye, but Frankie appeared deeply interested in the ancient story and Mrs. Wilson's notes on the chalkboard. At noon, Frankie sat down with her lunch-bag next to Brenda Larson, who wore wrinkled plaid dresses and normally sat alone in the rec-room with a book open before her on the table. Rebecca and Shirley sat across from one another. Shirley left space on the end of her bench for Rafael, only as a courtesy Rebecca knew, because angels were not bodily figures, not exactly, and they had no need to sit.

Around other tables in the school's rec-room sat the girls who Rafael said were in trouble: Miranda, Mary, Julie, Patricia, Sarah, Dorothy and Gloria. Gloria was with her boyfriend, slow-talking and clumsy-footed Arthur Smith. If Gloria was in trouble, it seemed unlikely that Arthur was responsible. Yet Rafael's claims were too fantastic to be true, that Henry—or rather Henry's spirit, his ghost in other words—had visited the girls in their beds, in their unwaking hours even (Rafael often used odd phrases like that, *unwaking hours*), and lay with them and now each was with child. Henry Goodpath had been on a tractor, mowing the grass in Hewitts' field, when the old Minne-Moline turned over on a steep slope and Henry was killed. Mrs. Hewitt found him when he hadn't come in for lunch. That had been nearly two years ago.

Rebecca thought of the terror of becoming pregnant, the shame of it. Still, there was part of her that registered the hurt of being passed over by Henry's spirit, or rather it aggravated the old wound of being the girl that none of the boys noticed. Frankie's attention had done a lot to make up for that hurt. She looked over at Frankie, who was laughing at a joke she and one of her new lunch friends had shared. In her merriment, she quickly looked and found Rebecca's eye. Scalded, the girls turned away.

Δ

FRANKIE'S DREAM: There is a long corridor, the floor reflective with wax. Along one side are windows, along the other, nothing—it is immaterial: a corridor with only one side. It is bright, the light intense. She walks along the bright hall with a vague sense that she is late to be somewhere, an appointment that carries with it an equally vague sense of dread. Something catches her attention, and she looks to the right. A pair of children are outdoors playing tetherball. One child is too small and the rubber ball on the rope orbits over her head, out of reach; it is pointless to try. She tries to see who the tall child and the small child are but their faces are turned away. She looks through the next window and the scene is changed: it is only an empty courtyard of grass and leafy bushes. She walks farther. She can smell the wax on the floor, tart like blood oranges. A voice calls to her, "Francine," the name her mother uses, used to . . . she recalls that she is gone, like geese in winter, but with a never-coming spring. The voice grows louder. She stops and peers out the window. Rebecca is standing close to it, her face nearly against the pane. She calls, "Francine!" Rebecca is in a white dress, like a baptismal gown, her leaf-brown hair curled in unkempt ringlets. Rebecca appears anxious. She knows that she should relieve her friend's anxiety and call back to her but remains mute. Rebecca calls again, "Francine!" Behind her, the children's voices cry out as if panicked. She leaves Rebecca at the window to check on

16

the children playing tetherball. They and Rebecca should be in the same courtyard, yet they are not. She returns to the children's window and they are gone. The tethered ball bumps against its pole in the wind that has risen. A terrible storm of scab-colored clouds has sprung up and is approaching with malice. She realizes that Rebecca is in danger and tries to rush back to where she left her standing. The wax on the floor has softened and become sticky, clinging to her bare feet. It requires great effort to lift them. Meanwhile the storm approaches, nearer and nearer. Outside the wind sweeps across the bushes, which vibrate as if with current. Finally she reaches Rebecca's window, and her friend has moved away and is standing in the courtyard with her back to her. She may be watching the terrible storm or may be oblivious to it. She tries to open the window but it is shut tight, as if nailed in place. Her panic grows as she struggles with the immovable window. It may not be Rebecca at all in the courtyard, the wind slashing at the whipping white dress—it may be her mother, whose voice she cannot recall even in dreams. **Rebecca's dream**: She seems to hear the rhythmic squeal of the rusty chain for a long while before realizing it's the chain on the swingset grating against the bolts which secure it. She pulls hard with her arms to propel herself in a greater and greater arc. The old chain is cold and rough with rust in her hands, the wooden seat slick with age and use. The skirt of her dress, white like an innocent child's gown, billows with air at each forward thrust, then flattens with backward momentum. She is in an enormous green park with nothing but grass—no trees or bushes or flowers. In the far distance is a large building of brown brick, like a factory or a big-city high school. Where has everyone gone? It is an unimportant question. She is calm and content, except for the grating chain, which grows louder the higher she is able to swing. She strains to go higher even though she could fly off the age-slick seat. Her father is before her standing in the park wearing his minister's black with the white collar, clothes he saves for weddings and funerals. He is calmly watching her, a faint smile on his thin lips. They stay like that—she swinging and her father watching for a long while, contented. "Catch me, Daddy!" He raises his hands but he is farther away. At the conclusion of the next arc farther still. "Closer, Daddy!" His smile is just as benevolent but he continues to be more distant, and more distant, hands upraised as they are every Sunday toward Jesus on the cross, his back to the congregation. Panicked, she feels herself slipping from the seat. She mustn't wait any longer for her father to come to her. She releases herself into the still air. **Wendell Phillips's dream**: The congregants sit bovinely in the pews watching their pastor, truly with the blank expression of the cattle on Frank Whittle's farm. He adjusts his black-rimmed glasses, straightens the knot of his necktie, glances down at the Scripture before him, and reads aloud, "When he disembarked and saw the vast crowd, his heart was moved with pity for them, for they were like sheep without a shepherd . . ." He glances up at the congregation and is startled by a strange light emanating from the pews. He thinks for a second that he has neglected to turn on the sanctuary's overhead fixtures when he arrived and someone has finally realized and flipped the switch; but he immediately dismisses the idea. The sudden glow is coming from the congregants themselves. The pastor squints against the oncoming glare: specifically the light comes from an aura cast by each of the teenage girls— white light tinged in rose or ice blue or blushing lavender, framing their lovely heads. And the radiance queerly lights and shades the other members of the congregation, transforming their features into light and dark masks as intricate and mysterious as the moon's cratered and peaked shadows. The weird glow backlights the girls' faces, making it difficult to identify who is who. But neither the haloed girls nor the others seem to be aware of their nimbuses. The pastor has quit reading and is blinking against the harsh glare when just as suddenly the illumination ceases . . . and he realizes his congregants are staring at him quizzically. He issues a wan smile and recovers his place in Mark. **Shirley's dream**: Rafael smells like cloves, freshly chopped; Bertram an old dog damp from the rain; Charles an ear of corn freshly shucked; Damien the waxed floor near a boiler, hot in winter; Daniel chrysanthemum petals freshly picked and rubbed between the fingers; Edgar red brick still warm from the kiln; Edward sweat from a private recess of the body on the warmest of days; Frederic pine cones popping in an autumn fire; Garth chicory brewed in boiling water; Gerald a green apple cored before cutting; Henry cinnamon bathed in melting butter; John the pages of old books finally open after long-absent readers; Kristopher forsythia blossoms blown by a spring storm; Liam black earth spaded over, its insect world suddenly exposed to light; Marcus the musk of damp wool; Orlando the zest of blood oranges; Philip spring grass, newly mowed of a dewy morning; Samuel wild onions on the breeze in midsummer; Terrance the dust trapped in pine drawers; Theodore pumpkin pulp scooped in preparation of carving; Ulysses minced meat filling upon perforating the paraffin; Xanther, cucumber water, iced and in the shade; Zane the red wine of sacrament; Anthony English aftershave and the smoke of Pall Malls.

E

Frankie propped the bed pillows behind her back, pulled over the flowered spread so that it covered her legs, and took up the book on her side table, the library's copy of the *Odyssey*. It was a thick volume with green binding, old and often-read. She appreciated its smell and its feel as much as its words. Frankie felt exhausted, and she knew it was from the stress of losing Rebecca's friendship. Since her mother's death, when Frankie was eleven, she had not allowed herself to become close to anyone—to love anyone—because the pain of loss was too great and too thorough. It crept into all your corners, seeped through all the cracks, and wormed its way into the very marrow of your heart. It was only now at her loss that Frankie knew she loved Rebecca—the pain she felt proved it, like cornstarch sprinkled on an oily thumbprint reveals it and all of its contours, plain as day. She sat on her bed for a time and explored the contours of her loss, the curvatures of her hurt.

She opened the book to the part they had mainly studied in class: the hero's communion with the dead. They only had an excerpt in their school textbook, and Frankie wanted to read the entire section. The story touched her pain, inflaming it where it so long had lain hidden, giving her pain a concreteness, a shape and a substance, thus easing some of the terror of it, like a menace that has lingered in the shadows at last coming into the light.

Frankie gradually came to understand these things, in

some recessed space of her mind, as she read about the Greek soldier's entrance into the murky underworld. The ghosts came upon him, thirsty for the blood of sacrifice he'd spilt in the gloom. Mrs. Wilson, their English teacher, said that the hero had survived ten years of horrific warfare, and one way of reading his account of his travels home is that of a man whose soundness of mind had been compromised—*by death in continual close quarters*, that's how Mrs. Wilson had put it. She didn't want to say Odysseus was mad, not so plainly, because Mrs. Wilson's brother had come back from Korea *not right* (everyone knew it but hardly anyone said), and he'd only been home for a while before moving away again. Maybe to Chicago. That was the story.

Frankie used the bed cover to blot the tears from her cheeks as she read of the Greek's encountering his mother in the underworld, in fact learning of her death that way. Odysseus wept too—each in sympathy with the other, for all their losses.

Z

FRANKIE WOKE IN THE NIGHT, wondered at the time, and tried to fall back asleep. She'd had strange dreams but couldn't recall their details, yet they'd left their strangeness upon her. She pulled back the covers and untangled her legs from her sleeping gown. Moonlight was etched on the curtain in her bedroom, which drew her to the window. She walked on tiptoe in an effort to avoid the chill of the wood floor.

There was a person standing on the walk before her house, and she recognized Rebecca's form immediately in the moon's indigo-tinted light. There appeared to be a second person with Rebecca, someone largely shielded by her friend's body and obscure in spite of the moonlight. Rebecca waved up at Frankie and motioned toward the side of the house.

Frankie nodded and stepped back from the window, letting the curtain close. For a moment she considered leaving Rebecca standing at her door, as she had been left standing at Shirley's. She suspected it was Shirley who accompanied Rebecca, which made the opportunity for payback more than twice as tempting.

Frankie took her robe from the foot of the bed, and began to make her way downstairs. She paused for a moment at her father's half-open door and confirmed his quiet snoring. She walked through the dark living room and didn't switch on a lamp until she came to the kitchen. Rebecca hadn't knocked but she assumed she was standing outside the kitchen door, she and Shirley.

Frankie used one finger to pull back the curtain over the door's window, and she saw a single dark figure in profile, who then turned toward the window and offered a little wave to her friend.

Frankie opened the door and Rebecca stepped inside. Frankie peered about the night for Shirley, perhaps embarrassed to come forward, as she shut the door. She turned, What's going on?

Rebecca's blue wool coat was buttoned over her school dress, as if she hadn't been to bed. It wasn't as cold tonight as it had been but Rebecca seemed chilled. She wore gray wool socks pulled up to her knees, so that only her pale kneecaps showed beneath the hem of her dress.

It's good to see you, said Rebecca.

Frankie realized her friend was nearly at the point of tears. In fact, her eyes were red and raw as if she'd already been crying—perhaps finally sorry for the way she'd been treating her. If that's what was happening here—and Frankie ached for it to be—she wasn't quite ready to forgive her.

It's late, Frankie said, hugging herself as if she was chilled too when in fact she was oppressively warm with agitation.

Yes, I'm sorry . . . I wasn't sure I should come. . . .

But here you are. Frankie walked past her friend, pulled a kitchen chair out at an angle and sat.

Rebecca went to the table also and stood with her hands on the back of a chair. Frankie didn't invite her to sit down.

Why've you come? We have to be quiet, Daddy's asleep.

I have to tell you something (almost in a whisper), but I can't say everything.

You're not making sense. Frankie wanted to shout it. She felt her anger and hurt churning up from someplace deep within her, a place until that moment she didn't know

23

existed. She swallowed hard to try to keep the emotions from erupting.

Rebecca fidgeted with a button on her coat. How have you been, how've you been feeling?

You came here at this hour to ask me that? You could ask me that at school—if you were talking to me. Frankie pulled her robe tight around her stomach and chest. She felt the tears coming but the last thing she wanted was to cry, to let Rebecca know how deeply she'd hurt her—though she obviously knew.

No, said Rebecca, it's not just that . . .

What then?

More fidgeting with the button, a new habit, Frankie decided. I, began Rebecca, have information . . . She began again: I know that you . . . More fidgeting.

For the love of God, spit it out! Frankie tried to check her voice at the last.

You're going to have a baby, blurted Rebecca, nearly pulling her button from her coat.

Frankie stared at her friend. What are you talking about?

You need to see Dr. Higgins, or someone—*there's a baby inside you.*

That's insane, that's impossible. You need to have The Talk again. Yet all at once the idea saturated Frankie's thoughts—and the things she'd been experiencing lately, the tiredness, the sadness, the sense that she was one step away—one insult, one rude look, one stubbed toe—from exploding, or from weeping and dissolving. Why do you say that? Frankie quickly stood and placed her hands on the back of her chair.

Rebecca tried to reach over and touch Frankie's hand but she suddenly put her hands in the pockets of her robe.

You'd better go. It's late.

I'm sorry to upset you, said Rebecca as she turned toward the door. Frankie neither moved nor spoke as Rebecca let herself out.

H

REBECCA HAD GOTTEN AS FAR as the street before the tears returned. A whisper of winter was still in the chill wind. Her tears turned cold as they ran down her cheeks. She felt a chaos of emotions whirling within her: shame, frustration, the anger bred of frustration, rejection, weakness. She took a hanky from the pocket of her coat, wiped her nose, and began walking toward home.

She told her father that she was spending the night at Shirley's—they'd be up late working on their history project—and she told Shirley that her father had chores for her at home, all of which contributed guilt to her tempest of emotions. She walked the quiet streets in no rush to get home. She wanted time to think, to try to sort out her thoughts, which seemed like fallen leaves caught in a sudden storm, swirling, flying every which way. She recalled how excited she was when she learned of the angels, and how excited Shirley was to tell her about them. Day by day Shirley told Rebecca more and more about the troupe of angels who surrounded her, the details becoming more and more precise.

But along with the excitement there was the anxiety and sadness of keeping secrets from Frankie, whom she wanted to tell about the angels but Shirley insisted they must be their secret. This was different though. Frankie was in trouble and deserved to know, sooner rather than later, perhaps soon enough to do something about it. Rebecca tried to ignore that her mind had jumped to that possibility, to forget that she could be a party to anything like that.

Why then had she gone to Frankie in the night? What had she hoped to accomplish, if not to set that possibility in motion?

These questions remained half-formed and unspoken in her heart, yet left the traces of unarticulated echoes.

She'd been walking slowly. She realized she was near the square, which was dominated by the gazebo, whitewashed in moonlight. She recalled the morning last summer that she and Frankie sat in the gazebo. It was an oppressively hot day, and a bee buzzed along the gazebo's rafters, as if trapped inside the open structure. Rebecca barely knew Frankie then, and on that morning she was irritated with her frankness, a quality they came to call her *Frankieness* when their friendship blossomed.

Rebecca stopped and looked directly at the gazebo, perhaps hoping to see the ghosts of their younger selves still haunting its shadowed interior. She was surprised to discern a dark figure standing among the shadows, watching her it seemed. He stood so still it was possible to think he wasn't there at all, just a trick of the light and the dark.

In fact the longer she watched, only a few seconds, the more she convinced herself there was no one there at all. She thought of calling out to him but preferred the idea that the gazebo was abandoned.

Rebecca put her hands in her pockets and continued walking toward home. She tried to put it all out of her mind—Shirley and the angels, Frankie's anger and hurt, and the trouble her friend was in, her father's moodiness of late and the strain it was causing her mother—and focus on something else. She thought of school, where she understood the problems put before her: finding the area of a triangle, solving for *x*, listing the major battles of the

Civil War, knowing whose assassination started the Great War, identifying the anatomical features of an earthworm, recognizing trees by the shape of their leaves, conquering the chord shifts in *Moonlight Sonata*, baking a pie so that the apples stay firm but not hard, knowing the proper way to respond to a boy when he invites you to dance . . . if one ever would.

Then there was Mrs. Wilson's class, and the stories and poems they were assigned to read. There was some information she could commit to memory, which author wrote which piece, when the authors were born and when they died, but the stories and poems themselves were slippery. They had meaning but Mrs. Wilson wasn't inclined to tell them what it was. Instead they were supposed to grope around, inside the sentences and lines, the paragraphs and stanzas, stumbling toward meaning on their own.

She thought of the poem by Homer, about the Greek soldier and his wanderings from fantastic place to fantastic place—the island of the wind-god, the land of the cannibals, the coastline of the beautiful and dangerous women, and especially she thought of the underworld of the dead. He had to find the blind prophet who would advise him how to reach home. Mrs. Wilson suggested that because the Greek had been in that terrible war with the Trojans for all those years, ten years, that perhaps he wasn't visiting the dead, not really, that they were just a product of his imagination—*his wrecked imagination*, Mrs. Wilson called it.

Rebecca came to the corner of her street, Willow, turned and stopped. She thought that she'd been hearing footsteps which weren't quite in sync with her own, and there they were for a second before stopping too. She peered down the long brick walk of Main Street, its darkness broken here and there by even darker shadows.

The wind kicked up for a moment and it carried with

it the smell of cigarettes mixed with, competing with, sweet-scented cologne. For a brief second Rebecca believed she saw the form of a man on the walk but it may have only been a trick of the overlapping shadows.

She hurried along Willow Street, nearly running, feeling both foolish and afraid. Convinced that the man was following her, she didn't dare look back. She reached her front gate and rushed faster still until she was inside her house. She shut the door harder (louder) than she might, and she bolted the door, which was never bolted. There were two diamond-shaped panes in the door but they were made to give only a blurred view of the world. She had to rise onto her toes to peer out one of them. Perhaps someone was at the gate, or it was only the shadows of limbs falling across the glass.

Rebecca?

She turned, startled. Yes, Daddy, it's me. The stairs were dark but she imagined he was at their top in his pajamas. I'm not feeling well, and I didn't want to get Shirley sick.

Be sure to gargle before you go to bed.

Yes, Daddy. She heard him return to bed, his parental duty performed. She took a last look through the blurring window and was surprised by a splash of light on the pane. She was confused by what she saw until she heard the growl of thunder: the first storm of spring.

⊖

SHIRLEY TRIED DRINKING WARM MILK before bed but it did little good and she spent most nights awake. Having Rebecca over provided some comfort, though not much more sleep. The activities of the angels, their comings and goings, and their incessant talking, made it nearly impossible. It mattered not whether it was dark or light, Shirley saw them just as plainly. In the dark, the angels carried their own radiance, not a radiance that fell upon other things but it was like they were unaffected by darkness.

So as Shirley lay in bed, the lamp next to her switched off to make her parents think she was sleeping, she watched the angels and listened to their conversations, nearly all meaningless to her. **Rafael** stood by her bed, from time to time speaking to one of his fellows or commenting to Shirley. Rafael had dark hair and darker features. He wore a long shirt of crimson velvet tied at the waste with a golden sash. His black pants stopped at his knees and beneath were black stockings and black leather shoes with heels that added a few inches to his height. He often kept his fingers tucked into the sash with only his thumbs resting free. **Marcus** wore a gray wool coat with large buttons carved of bone, and trousers of darker and lighter gray stripes, gathered into tall black boots. His hair was as dark as Rafael's but his long, narrow face was much paler beneath a thin black beard. He tended to speak with his hands, and when they weren't gesturing excitedly, his arms were folded tightly across his chest—the position they would be brought to for dramatic emphasis after declaring his irritation at some modern mechanical noise. **Philip** walked with a limp and a hand on the hip of his bad leg nearly at all times, rendering himself in effect a double cripple. He wore a suit which had the cut of a military uniform, though there were no signet patches or epaulettes or sashes. His black hair and beard were neatly trimmed. Of all the angels he seemed particularly interested in the card game that Rafael directed Shirley's hand to play. **Terrance** was one of the strangest angels and at first frightened her but she'd grown accustomed to him. He was dressed in rags like a beggar and kept apart from the others. He was blind, and in fact his lids were sunken and shadowed, suggesting he had no eyes beneath them. His age-spotted hands remained clasped at his stomach. His unkempt hair and beard were gray-white. He continually spoke to himself in a quiet whisper. She once stood near him for a long while trying to hear what he was saying. She heard words but their patterns formed no meaning for her.

The activities of the angels were continuous. If Rebecca was there, Shirley would put her face against her friend's shoulder, and Rebecca would cradle her head, at least partly shutting out the angels, their movements and conversations, and she could sleep for a while. Without Rebecca she was especially restless, at one point even burying her head beneath her pillow. Shortly she gave up and sat with her back against the headboard.

Her father didn't have chores for her, Rafael said quietly.

Shirley turned to him, bearing his own light in the dark bedroom.

You know that already.

I don't know any such thing. She said her father wanted her home, and he wanted her home.

Rafael was silent but his look nagged her.

All right then. Where is she?

Rafael spoke to Marcus, nonsense about how the weather would be turning.

I'm sorry, Rafael. Where has Rebecca gone tonight?

He hesitated, defiant also. You know that too.

Shirley watched the luminous angels, whose numbers had suddenly doubled. Frankie . . . Rebecca had returned to Frankie. She always knew it would happen. Rebecca had turned away from her when Frankie and her father moved to the village, but she came back to her when she told her about the angels. She knew it was fleeting. Frankie had some hold on her—she had a hold on almost everyone in the village. She saw the way the boys and men watched her, even in church, after the children's blessing, even Rebecca's father. It was disgusting. Frankie pretended not to notice, but she ate it up, like thick-frosted birthday cake.

We should go there too. Tell her how it makes you feel, to be abandoned again.

It wasn't right, to go to Frankie's house at this hour to confront Rebecca. It wasn't right but the idea burned inside her, deep—perhaps in the place that is her soul. The angels became especially noisy and numerous, crowding her, making it difficult to breathe. She was sick to her stomach, and she felt a terrible pressure and ache behind her eyes.

Shirley threw off her bedcovers. She was still wearing her robe over her pajamas. She weaved her way through the angels, most of whom paid her no attention. She had to stop to pick up her shoes near the blind angel dressed in rags. When she raised up he was *looking* directly at her with his sightless sunken lids. He'd ceased his meaningless muttering. His breath smelled of onions and a spice she had no name for. She never left the house, Terrance said . . . then turned away to continue his whisperings.

Shirley stopped in the kitchen long enough to put on her shoes. Then she slipped out of the kitchen door, careful not to let the screen-door bang shut. The night was cool and something on the breeze hinted of a coming storm, one that would wash away the remnants of winter. She went to the garage, which was her father's domain, and entered through the side door. It was a cramped space, taken up mainly with the family Ford Galaxie, but her father had a small worktable in one corner, and above it hung a safety-light on a black cord. Shirley felt her way in the familiar dark, one hand before her and the other on the cold metal of the car, until she reached the light and switched on the harsh bulb. She squinted against the painful glare.

Sometimes her father would get angry at her mother and at Shirley and her brother—over the smallest things, or nothing at all. He would get that look, something about the corners of his eyes, and his lips, straight across like he was pressing something between them, pressing hard. Then he'd go to the garage to be by himself, away from the family. Some weekends and evenings he spent nearly all his time there.

Shirley took down a Folgers coffee can from a shelf and removed the pack of Pall Malls her father kept there. The pack was open and half full. She took a cigarette and lit it with a match from the book also kept in the coffee can. She switched off the light and smoked in the dark, with only a thin beam from a streetlamp coming through a dirty pane of glass in the garage door. She snuck her first cigarette when she was twelve. When her nerves were buzzing, the rhythm of the long slow draws of smoke into her lungs was the only thing that would calm her. There were times that it was agonizing waiting for everyone to go to sleep so she could sneak out to the garage.

Rafael had of course come with her, and he stood watching the beam of streetlamp too.

After a while she was growing cold, so she took her father's old canvas coat from the peg where he kept it for working outside in cool weather. It was too big for her but its weight felt comforting on her shoulders, and the shearling collar smelled of her father's cologne, mixed pleasantly with a trace of the lamb's original musk.

She flicked ash on the floor of hard-packed earth and looked for a moment at the hand holding the cigarette between her fingers, the skin slightly sallow in the ray of streetlight. It didn't seem to be her hand at the end of the coat sleeve. The hand turned so that different fingers shone in light or in shadow, the smoke from the cigarette rising in the yellow light then sharply disappearing.

Shirley felt something running along her cheek like a fingertip. She looked at Rafael, who remained as still as stone, and she realized it was a tear that had trailed across her face. It gathered at the corner of her lips and she tasted its salt.

Other angels had joined Rafael and her in the garage, Marcus and Xanther and others. The space was too tight and Shirley felt again as if she couldn't breathe. She opened the door and hurried into the cool night air. For a moment she could catch her breath but she knew the angels would be upon her soon. More and more they came to her. She wanted Rafael to make them leave her be at school and church but he was quiet and raised no objections to them.

On the street, she tossed her cigarette into the gutter and began walking.

The dozen or so primary streets of the village were neatly arranged on a grid, like the paper they used at school to learn geometry, but once one went beyond the grid the streets transformed into roads and lanes, blacktops and highways; and then other rules governed their windings besides simple mathematics, conforming to boundaries of the landscape, the ownership of property, and the county's legislated needs. At the heart of the math was the village square, and at its heart the gazebo, ghostly white at the moment, lit by the moon, though increasing cloud cover meant to obscure the glowing disc.

Shirley was attracted to the gazebo's unearthly light, for it seemed like the light of the angels. As she walked Rafael was at her side, his radiance just at the edge of her vision. She climbed the steps of the gazebo, thinking that in summer the Passion would be performed there, the drama of the war between Heaven and Hell—and this year it would mean so much more to her. She imagined herself boldly coming forth from the audience, stepping past the adults who were playing the parts, ascending the gazebo's steps, turning—as she did now—and announcing the angels, testifying to their visitation to earth—to commune with *her*, unremarkable Shirley Donaldson.

And the angels would reveal their presence, one by one, to the wonderment of all who had gathered there, to the entire village. The rapture of it brought more tears to her eyes. The astonishment of everyone, especially her teachers and the girls at school who paid no attention to her, and her father. And they would ask her questions about the angels, when had they come to her, what was their purpose on earth. . . .

Rebecca would be there, silent, because she could have been part of the revelation, receiving everyone's awe nearly as much as Shirley—but Rebecca had abandoned her and the angels, denied them to return to Frankie.

Shirley's eyes burned with the hurt and the anger of denial. She rubbed them with the sleeve of her father's coat. As her vision cleared she saw a figure walking past the square. Rebecca, said Rafael at her side . . . or was it Rafael who spoke? His voice was altered, hoarser, reminding her of Anthony's, before Rafael had driven him away.

Rebecca, walking by, seemed to notice them in the gazebo, though they stayed as still as stone. Then she quickened her pace, maybe a little afraid, and Shirley was pleased. She and the angel waited a moment before leaving the gazebo and following her.

Shirley's feeling of betrayal was so poignant she wanted to lash out at Rebecca, to trip her, to pull her hair. She was coming from the direction of Frankie's house, and she was alone, which perhaps meant that Frankie had denied *her*. A taste of satisfaction tempered Shirley's hunger to do her friend harm. Still, they followed her, keeping their distance, keeping to the darkest shadows.

I

FRANKIE HADN'T EVEN GOTTEN UNDER THE COVERS when she acknowledged to herself that it would be fruitless to go back to bed. She'd been waiting for Rebecca to come to her for so long—and when she finally did, it had all gone wrong. The anger and the hurt she felt came out only as anger . . . a petty, cruel anger. Perhaps the anger had been exorcised from her soul, somewhat, but the hurt was still there, burning painfully, and now she added shame at the way she'd treated Rebecca.

Her corduroy pants were folded over the chair in her bedroom. She slipped them on, tucking her sleeping gown into them. Downstairs, she pulled on her coat and boots, then quietly opened the kitchen door.

Moonlight mixed with the breeze, which hinted at a coming storm. She turned in the direction of Rebecca's house. What if, instead, Rebecca had gone to the Donaldsons'? There was no purpose in considering the possibility. A better question was what was she doing at all?

The streets were quiet, deserted. It seemed the entire village was asleep except for Rebecca and her. Many were the nights Frankie lay in bed feeling that way: that she was the only wakeful person in the world. It was so comforting to hear Rebecca sleeping next to her in the twin bed, to feel her leg and hip and shoulder pressed against her own leg and hip and shoulder. Rebecca's sinking down next to her in bed, with the heat of her body rising and radiating through her, filled a space left vacant since the loss of her mother, which also marked the loss of her brother—the brother she never knew except as the bearer of her mother's death. She tried not to think of the baby in that way, to remind herself, rather, of his innocence, but the baby and death were forever intertwined, like that black-and-white Oriental symbol of the two fish wrapped around each other.

Frankie didn't comprehend how large the emptiness was that Rebecca had been filling until Rebecca was no longer filling it, and in fact her absence added its own emptiness to the terrible void. Frankie wanted to find Rebecca and somehow explain these feelings to her—why hadn't she tried when Rebecca was standing in her kitchen? Why had she been mute with anger, muzzled by a seething rage? Those feelings were gone now, leaving in their place only the exhaustion of having borne them.

The night breeze seemed suddenly colder, more wedded to storm. Frankie turned up her coat collar and began walking toward Rebecca's. She had only set off when lightning traced across the western sky, followed momentarily by a muttering of thunder. Perhaps it was a bad decision to be out but now she was set on the idea of seeing Rebecca. She was driven by a longing as if she hadn't been with her for many months, for years—and she thought of Odysseus, separated from his wife for twenty years, and her desire to be with Rebecca felt as keen and as prickled as the Greek soldier's.

Frankie's reverie was such that she'd been walking without thinking of her path, and she found herself near the square: another spasm of lightning flooded upon the white gazebo, then was gone. An icy drop of rain struck Frankie on the cheek, and another, and another. Instinctively she rushed to the gazebo for shelter. Inside, rain sounded like pebbles pelting its roof. The wind had risen and carried a cold spray to Frankie's face and hands. She thought that if she hadn't been so frigid to Rebecca, she may have stayed long enough to be caught at Frankie's by the rain—affording them the chance to make right their differences, and due to the lateness, they may have weathered the storm in Frankie's bed.

But instead here she was, cold and alone, perhaps with Rebecca driven back to Shirley's, to lay snug beneath *her* covers, holding hands and whispering above the rain.

Lightning revealed a figure in the square rushing toward the gazebo. In the glimpse he appeared to be a man, in a man's coat, head down. Frankie was startled and had no time to do anything beyond that reaction. The figure bounded up the gazebo's steps, probably only then realizing someone else was there.

The breeze flared and Frankie smelled cigarettes and shave cologne. The man was short, with long wet hair that clung to his face, and beneath the old jacket a wet skirt hung below his knees, like a gown in Doc Higgins's office—in all, making the impression he was an escaped mental patient (there was just such a hospital in Crawford).

The strange man seemed to be sizing up Frankie too, in these first few seconds of their encounter, standing facing one another. Lightning illuminated the square and their two profiles. As the flash fluttered the man rushed at Frankie, grabbing her hair with one hand and pushing her back with the other. Their legs tangled and they both slipped on the gazebo's wet floor, landing hard on their shoulders. Frankie had omitted a little animal cry of surprise and fear that was lost in the ripple of thunder.

The man clutched the collar of Frankie's coat with one hand but Frankie was able to jerk herself free and scramble backward until her back bumped into the gazebo's railing.

Her attacker started to get up but immediately crumpled onto his side again, clutching the shoulder he'd landed on. He rolled onto his back moaning in pain.

Frankie thought it was her moment to escape but in a flash of lightning she realized that her attacker was even smaller than she'd thought, and before the ensuing thunder she heard him crying. Frankie crawled to him and pushed the wet hair from his face, a face she knew.

What are you doing, Shirley? Are you hurt?

But Shirley Donaldson didn't respond, in fact, didn't seem to know that Frankie was there at all.

Frankie looked out across the square and the rain had already let up. She looked down again: Stay here. I'll get help. You may have knocked your shoulder out of joint.

Rebecca's house was closest, and Pastor and Mrs. Phillips would know what to do—Frankie sensed that Shirley needed more than Doc Higgins's tending. Between sobs Shirley spoke to someone but not, it seemed, to Frankie.

Frankie stepped cautiously down the wet steps and hurried toward Rebecca's. When she reached the walk bordering the square, rain still falling, she looked back at the gazebo. For a half second it appeared there were several people in the gazebo but their dark and distorted shapes dissolved into a labyrinth of shadows with the next fissure of lightning.

About the Author

TED MORRISSEY is the author of seven works of fiction, including, most recently, *Crowsong for the Stricken* and the forthcoming *Mrs Saville*. His novella *Weeping with an Ancient God* was a *Chicago Book Review* Best Book of 2015, and his stories and novel excerpts have appeared in more than fifty journals, among them *Glimmer Train Stories*, *PANK*, *ink&coda*, and *Southern Humanities Review*. A Ph.D. in English studies, he has also published two works of scholarship. In addition to teaching high school English, he is a lecturer in Lindenwood University's MFA in Writing program (online). Previous to that he was a lecturer in English at Benedictine University and University of Illinois, Springfield campuses. His wife Melissa is an educator and children's author. Together they have five adult children, one grandchild, and two rescue dogs. Ted founded Twelve Winters Press in 2012, modeling it after Leonard and Virginia Woolf's Hogarth Press.

tedmorrissey.com

@t_morrissey (Twitter)

jtedmorrissey (Facebook)

tedmorrissey (YouTube)

Afterword

Adapting the novella for audio, stage and screen

Jenny Bacon

THE CURVATURES OF HURT resides in the molten lava core of the hearts of adolescence, a constantly shifting terrain; it exists in the space where omnipotence and powerlessness collide, the fault line of development when you really become who you are, and friendships are more than what the time-space continuum can hold. The three young women that Ted Morrissey has created seem to breathe on their own; they are so carefully drawn that you are a little bit afraid that they might look back out at you from the page, and be startled and run away, never to be seen again. Reading the story for the audiobook was always like reading a mystery, for the first time.

Stage work happens on a scale that is much broader than audio; quite simply, the audience is farther away. You are working as part of a larger team to create an image: for example, the lighting design, the sound design, the other performers, the specific challenges of the particular space inside which the performance is viewed. Additionally, the stage experience is ephemeral, and only happens once, never to be recreated in exactly the same way ever again.

In audio, you are literally trying to recreate a vacuum.

43

You have no control of the context in which your performance will be absorbed. Your performance will most likely be interrupted and influenced by factors completely beyond your imagination. And it is extremely intimate, like an Asian miniature painted with an eyelash.

Ted's work lends itself to this intimate medium particularly well, zooming in and out of the thoughts and perceptions of the characters while maintaining a consistent overall atmospheric experience. In transferring to another medium, I would consider it essential to maintain the feeling of magic that pervades the piece, that any moment reality will crack (the Angels are a rift, not a full-blown crack—as Shirley's experience indicates, the angels exist alongside reality). For example, the rain storm that comes near the end of the story: it seems to me that the potential storm has been present throughout the story, but when do we notice it? And when do the characters notice it? How does the storm become present for each character?

I would strongly advise a stage adaptation that relies on a creative and imaginative representation of the external world, to be able to keep it as fluid as possible. I am less versed in film technique from a director's standpoint, but my feeling from being inside the piece is that visceral, tactile experience should be maximized, the feeling of cold, the feeling of wet, the small details of a person's face, and a pervading sense of roiling under the surface. Their internal lives and their emotions are like this storm, utterly out of their control it seems to them; and yet, they have an expectation of being able to wrest control of others, the people they love.

Each girl has a tentative grasp of her own power; they are all on the cusp of awakening. One of the things I most appreciate about this story is that the awakening does not focus on the approval of boys or men (although it is not absent, certainly, and obviously plays an essential role for each girl) but that they are struggling to define their most intimate identity, and the bond they feel that they cannot survive this transition without is the one they form with each other.

Each girl's actions is consistent with her voice; Frankie's confidence, revealing her need, standing blatantly outside Shirley's house at the beginning, Rebecca's need for approval as she balances her lies against her loyalty when she sneaks to Frankie's house, Shirley's terror to maintain contact with reality as she obsesses the details of the angels who plague her, and even the doubts that are voiced in the Pastor's dream—these are people who lean on each other for their identities, none whole without the others.

Jenny Bacon has been performing profession-ally for many years. She has created characters in the room with some of the masters of the American Theater, among them Sam Shepard, Tony Kushner, Sarah Ruhl, Theresa Rebeck, Lisa Kron, David Rabe, and many others. She has worked with groundbreaking directors to execute their vision, Ivo van Hove, JoAnne Akalaitis, Daniel Aukin, Walter Bobbie, Robert Falls, Mary Zimmerman, Daniel Fish, Christopher Ashley, Leigh Silverman, and many, many others, garnering awards across America and a Herald Angel Award from the Edinburgh Festival. She has appeared on American television playing a variety of unfortunate souls in horrific circumstances, and, she says, has had an absolutely wonderful time doing it. Visit her at www.jcrispybacon.com.

To listen to Jenny Bacon's haunting vocal performance of *The Curvatures of Hurt*, purchase on Audible, Amazon and iTunes.

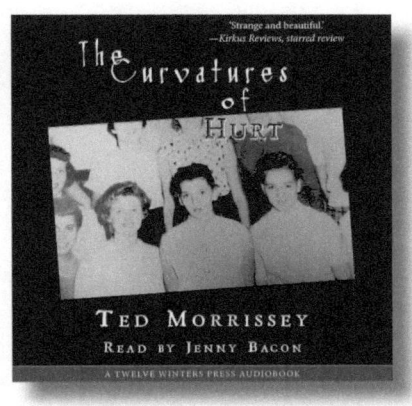

The Curvatures of Hurt is part of Ted Morrissey's prismatic novel *Crowsong for the Stricken*, available in hardcover, paperback and Kindle editions from Twelve Winters Press.

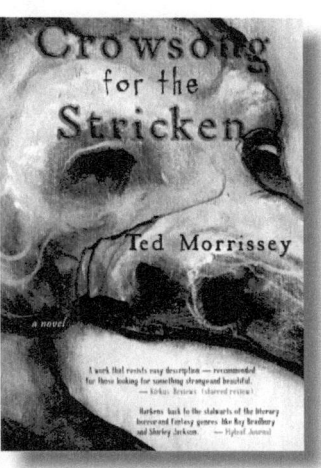

'A work that resists easy description — recommended for those looking for something strange and beautiful.'
— *Kirkus Reviews* (starred review)

'The language and the overall tone harken back to stalwarts of the literary fantasy and horror genres like Ray Bradbury and Shirley Jackson.'
— *Flyleaf Journal*

Also by Ted Morrissey
from Twelve Winters Press

'An enticing read . . . It stands as a great little
work of existential crisis and isolation.'
— *Chicago Book Review*
A CBR Best Book of 2015

'A haunting journey through mid-19th-century
London . . . an engrossing mystery.'
— *North American Review*

www.ingramcontent.com/pod-product-compliance
Lightning Source LLC
Chambersburg PA
CBHW020602130626
46552CB00007B/3006